JIM KNIGHTHORSE SERIES

Dark Horse
The Mummy Case
Hail Mary
Clean Slate
Easy Rider (short story)

EASY RIDER

////

J.R. RAIN

Published by
Crop Circle Books
212 Third Crater, Moon

Printed in the United States of America.

ISBN- 9798513615248

Dedication
To the memory of my father, who became a
Knighthorse fan at the end.
As Knighthorse would say, "Better late than
never."
Love you, pops.

1.

I try to get to work around nine.

Luckily, I have a very loose definition of *try* and *around*. And since I like to think of myself as *progressive*, I don't worry about things like *time*. That's the beauty of being progressive: I'll get there eventually.

At just past ten, I arrived at my building. With a mocha latte in one hand and my keys in the other, I smelled the cigarettes and cheap perfume wafting under my office door into the hallway.

Before slipping the key in the lock, I tested the handle. Still locked. I looked around me. My pathetic business complex was quiet. There were precisely four cars scattered around the parking lot. One of them was my van. The others might have been the same three cars I'd seen upon leaving my office yesterday.

Speaking of yesterday, I'd had precisely no clients come in, and had received exactly four calls from Bank of America credit card services. Apparently, I owed them a crap-ton of money. Apparently, they would get it when they got it. They didn't like that answer, of course, which might have been why they'd called three more times. I was looking forward to more such calls today.

Yippee!

My office is in Huntington Beach, but one would never guess it. It was too far away from the addictive, salt-laden ocean breeze. Too far away from the bikini babes. And definitely too far away from a steady stream of walk-in business.

One might assume that my office was on the wrong side of Huntington Beach, the inland side. It was the side that abutted a little city called Midway City. The side with, of course, the cheaper rent. Cheap or not, I was still two months behind on it.

Now as I slid the key into the lock and, balancing my mocha latte like a pro, I slipped my hand behind me and pulled out the Mossad's weapon of choice: a Walther pistol. I wasn't part of the Mossad. I wasn't a spy either. I was just a private investigator, and mostly, I wasn't even that. Mostly, I was an out-of-work desk jockey.

Now, as I opened my office door, I was certain someone had broken in...and was waiting for me inside.

***

My office isn't big, so there aren't many places for a man to hide. Or, in this case, a woman.

It turned out she wasn't doing a very good job of hiding, either. In fact, she was sprawled on my couch, sound asleep. I relaxed and slipped the gun back behind my back, just inside the waistband of my jeans. I studied the scene of the "crime." A coffee mug rested on the floor next to her, filled to overflowing with stubbed-out cigarettes. *My* coffee mug, in fact, which she'd commandeered from the cupboard over the small sink in the far corner of the office. Next to the sink sat an old, but reliable, Mr. Coffee. Or, as I liked to call it, *Señor Café*, because I liked to think of myself as international and mysterious. Kind of like James Bond, only bigger and tougher.

Anyway, the coffee mug was a favorite of mine. It also had the UCLA logo emblazoned across the side. I was one of those people who happened to think the UCLA logo should be emblazoned across most things, but I might have been in the minority.

Who she was, I didn't know. Why she had broken into my office and, from all appearances, why she had smoked the night away, I didn't know those answers either. I counted seventeen mostly smoked cigarettes, although one or two had only been smoked about halfway. I shook my head. *Wasteful.*

She looked to be about twenty-something. She might have also been cute, if not for the way she was presently drooling on the arm of my couch.

Speaking of arms, the inside of one of hers was covered with fresh track marks, all puckered and raw. Also on the inside of her arm was a stylized tattoo that said, "Fuck off, pigs."

I was impressed by the correct use of the comma.

There were many such tattoos covering her body. Or, at least, on the parts of her body that I could see. On her ankle there was a skull with a dagger through it. On her wrists were inked two roses, the stems of which dripped blood. Around her neck— yes, around her neck—was a barbed wire tattoo, also dripping blood. Behind both ears, turgid middle fingers flipped the bird.

Classy.

As badass as she wanted the world to think she was, all she was now was a gently snoring girl who'd broken into my office, abused one of my prized mugs, and was now staining my couch with her drool and cigarette stink.

Such is my life.

I also saw bruising, and not just a little bruising, but a lot. She'd been beaten recently. I suspected there were more such bruises covering other parts of her body that I couldn't see.

I might have felt weird about inspecting a sleeping woman so thoroughly; that was, if said sleeping woman hadn't broken into my office. I looked again at her mouth and saw the possible reason for all the drool...the inside of her lower lip was split. She'd taken a shot to the face. I noticed now how the blood mixed with the drool. Yes, I was going to have to get the couch cleaned. *Again.*

Don't ask.

How she'd broken into my office was a mystery. The mystery might have been solved if I'd gone through her purse, which was partly spilled open on the floor next to her. Two more unopened packs of cigarettes were visible inside the purse.

I always liked a woman who was prepared.

I stood back and considered my options. Call the cops? *Probably.* Wake her up?

Maybe. Check my email? *Definitely.*

So, while my unknown office guest slept contentedly, I powered up my computer and checked my email. I checked some sports scores. I checked my Facebook. Lastly, I checked my bank account.

Depressed, I did some triceps dips along the edge of my desk, as I'm sure most people the world over did. After all, who wouldn't want nice triceps?

Next, I did some diamond push-ups. Very few people know what a diamond push-up is. Even fewer know how to do them right. I'm one of the few who probably does them perfectly. Case in point, my hands were brought in together, centered just below my chest, my two index fingers and thumbs forming a perfect diamond. The burn is fabulous on both the triceps and the outer pecs. Since my focus was on the triceps this morning, I did just that: focused the burning in my triceps. I did push-up after push-up, cranking them out quickly, but precisely, over and over. I could do this until the cows came home, or until I got tired of them.

Or, in this case, until the mystery girl woke up on my couch, which she did now, gasping as she sat up.

However, I wasn't quite done with my diamond push-ups. No, no, no. My arms were burning, yes, but not burning *enough*. And so, I cranked out twenty-five more, knowing that I now had an audience.

When I was finished, I nodded to the woman who was now sitting up on the couch and watching me, her mouth hanging slightly open—and not because she had been recently beaten up. I think, perhaps, she might have been in awe. At least, I liked to think so.

"And that," I said, hopping up to my feet, "is how you do a diamond push-up."

"I don't know how to respond to that," she said.

"Few do," I said. "Now, start talking."

2.

I leaned a hip against my desk, arms folded over my still-burning chest.

The girl asked if she could smoke. I told her she couldn't. She pointed out that she'd smoked a crap-ton the night before, and what difference did it make? I pointed out that if people everywhere followed that line of logic, then the world would descend into anarchy. And if that happened, only the strong would survive...or those who had mastered the diamond push-up. She asked if I had been drinking. I told her I hadn't had a drink since last Tuesday. She looked skeptical.

"To sum up," I said, "the answer is no."

"Please."

"No."

"Pretty please?"

"There's nothing pretty about it. Start speaking. What's your name?"

"Camry," she said.

"Like the car?"

"Please don't make any Toyota jokes."

"I'm not sure I could if I tried."

"Well, good. I've heard a few corny ones, trust me." She pulled her sock-clad feet up on my couch and hugged her knees. Her socks were pristine white. How girls kept their socks so damn white was a mystery to me.

"Who are you?" I asked again.

"I told you."

"No, you told me your name, which just so happens to be the name of the most reliable car in America."

"Is that a joke?"

"Just an observation. Now, start talking."

She looked at me with eyes that weren't

fully awake, or alert, or aware. She might have been a little high. She was cute, in a strung-out kind of way. Dark rings around high cheekbones. Pale skin. Soft muscles hanging loose over a longish frame. She could have been beautiful. But for now, she had to settle for cute with a chaser of 'what could have been.'

"I need your help," she said finally. "But first, I would like some coffee."

I looked at her. She looked at me. Neither of us budged until I remembered her bruises and her bloody lip, which now hung in a pout. I sighed, pushed off the desk and headed over to the sink. Once there, I washed the coffee pot, slipped in a new filter, guesstimated the right amount of Folgers, and turned on *Señor Café*, which sounded more erotic than it should have.

While we waited, Camry was content to sit quietly on the couch, hugging her knees and looking forlorn. While the coffeemaker came to life, belching and hissing, I leaned against the little counter. A few years ago, I had tried to do incline push-ups against the little counter and had nearly torn the whole thing out of the wall.

"How did you get inside my office?" I finally asked.

For an answer, she reached inside her purse and pulled out a curious-looking gun-shaped tool that looked familiar. In fact, I had one in my desk drawer. It was a lock-pick gun.

"That would do it," I said, making a mental note to invest in a double-deadbolt for the door. "So you're a thief?"

She looked at me long and hard, although her eyes might have wavered a little. Being high does that. Finally, she nodded. "When I have to be."

"For drugs?"

"Is there another reason?" she asked.

"For the thrill of it?"

She shook her head and reached down for her pack of cigarettes, but as she did so, I shook my head and she sighed and dropped the pack back into her purse. "Sometimes, there's a thrill. Mostly, I'm terrified."

"You seemed real terrified," I said, "when I caught you drooling on my couch."

She snorted and wiped the corner of her

mouth. "Well, I wasn't robbing you. I was exhausted. It seemed like, you know, a safe place to crash. Besides, there's nothing here to rob."

"Ouch."

Behind me, my computer chimed. *An email.* It took all of my considerable will-power not to check it.

"How old are you?" I asked.

"Twenty-five."

"So, why are you here?"

"I need protection."

"From whom?"

She pushed up the sleeve of her shirt and showed me another tattoo. It was of a logo I was familiar with. Mostly I had seen it on the backs of leather jackets, worn by guys with long beards, long hair and loud motorcycles.

"From them."

J.R. RAIN

3.

Next, she asked if I had any food.

I held up my coffee cup and said, "You're looking at it."

She said, "Don't be mean," and started crying, and the next thing I knew I was in the drive-thru at Jack-in-the-Box, ordering her a breakfast croissant and juice, and for me, the entire left side of the menu.

Camry was asleep when I returned. I suspected the waterworks had been a ploy. Speaking of waterworks, yes, there was more drool. *Stay classy, Huntington Beach.*

I dropped her bag next to her and said,

"Breakfast."

She gasped and sat up. Chuckling, I went behind my desk and dug into my own two bags. Soon, we were making munching sounds.

"How did you hear about me?" I asked between sounds.

"I looked you up in an old phone book. I thought your name was the coolest one in the Yellow Pages."

"It is, and people still have those? Phone books?"

She didn't look at me while she ate. "Yes, why?"

I shrugged, although she didn't see me shrug. "I was making a social commentary on the progress of technology."

"Sounded more like a stupid question to me."

"That, too." I generally didn't take much to heart, especially from someone who was hungry, alone, hurting, and on the run. Whether or not she was a good person, I didn't much care. Whether or not I did my job right, kept her safe, and thwarted the evildoers, was a different story. "Do you want to talk about it?" I asked.

"About what?"

"Obamacare," I said. "Or why you need protection. You pick."

"You think you're funny or something?"

"Or something," I said.

"I don't think you're funny."

"Neither did Mrs. Neville."

"Who's that?"

"My sixth-grade teacher."

"If I tell you about it, will you stop with the jokes?"

"Probably not."

She thought about that as she munched on the last of the croissant sandwich I'd brought for her, a croissant sandwich that she'd yet to thank me for. After a moment, she shrugged and told me the story.

It had been a wild night of partying. In fact, every night was a wild night of partying. Camry was often high or drunk or both. She was Steel Eye's girl and everyone knew it and stayed away.

"Did you say Steel Eye?"

"Yes."

I nodded. "Carry on."

Everyone respected her and treated her as one of the guys. Except for one guy. One guy she had found interesting. One guy who was now dead. His name had been J-Bird.

"All we were doing was talking," said Camry, looking away and rubbing the back of her neck, "when Steel Eye flipped out."

"What else were you two doing?"

She did more neck-rubbing and shrugging, but now she wouldn't make eye contact with me. "We were maybe kissing, too."

"I take it Steel Toe didn't appreciate another man kissing his girl."

"Steel Eye, and yeah, you could say that."

"Did J-Bird understand the ramifications of kissing you?"

"He loved me. He would have done anything for me."

"Did you love him?"

She shrugged, looked away. "I thought he was interesting."

"You led him on."

"I might have flirted—"

"Did you encourage him?"

She shrugged. "I was bored."

"And now he's dead," I said. "Still bored?"

"No. Now, I'm scared."

I shook my head. "I think you knew what would happen to J-Bird. I think you knew that Steel Balls—"

"*Eye.*"

"—would come for J-Bird, probably even kill him. I don't think you cared much about the Birdman at all, because you were bored. I think you wanted some excitement. I think you got more excitement than you bargained for."

I watched her carefully. Her jaw rippled. She was angry. I watched her fists tighten around her napkin, the knuckles showing white. Then her hand opened a little and her jaw slackened. She looked at me with real tears in her eyes. It was a complete metamorphosis. "He promised to get me out of the gang. We talked quietly, secretly. For days. And one night we were both drinking and we got carried away."

I waited, watching her. Outside, something heavy rumbled along Beach Boulevard. The window in my office actually rattled. On the wall behind me, surrounding the window, were dozens of framed photographs and articles that featured yours truly. Back in the day, I was someone important. Now, I was only important to Cindy, my girlfriend, and Junior, my dog, which was good enough for me.

"But that didn't mean the son-of-a-bitch had to kill him. He fucking shot him. Right there."

"Did you see Steel Eye shoot him?"

"No. He'd slapped me. I was on the ground, crying. J-Bird tried to protect me from getting kicked and I heard them drag J-Bird away. Heard them beat him up pretty good. And then..."

"And then what?"

"They shot him in some bushes near the Pit."

"The Pit?"

"The fire pit we all hung out at."

"Of course," I said. "Because that's what bikers do, hang out in the desert around fire pits."

She said nothing. I didn't think she even heard me. After listening to her sobs and the steady drone of the afternoon traffic, I asked, "Where's the Pit?"

"What?"

"The Pit. Where's the Pit located?"

"The desert somewhere."

"What desert? Joshua Tree? Mohave? Serengeti?"

"I don't know. I just ride. I go where Steel Eye takes me."

"Is it in California?" I started the twenty questions game.

"Yes."

"What's the biggest city you can remember passing through?"

She thought about that for a long moment. "Palm Springs. Down the 111."

Yeah, there was a lot of desert around Palm Springs. Not a lot to go on, but I'd taken cases more vague than this.

"Any interesting scenery down that way?"

"The Salton Sea. There were pelicans. Wait, I do remember something." She paused. "There was a kitschy sign. It said, 'Slab City. Welcome.' Just after the sign was the turnoff we took. To the right. Dirt road goes right past the Pit."

Bingo. It only took three questions to get it out of her. I was that good. I knew the place, too. Slab City, a former military base, was now an RV squatters' town full of impromptu flea markets and drug commerce. Drifters and grifters.

I said, "What's Steel Eye's real name?"

"I don't know."

"What about J-Bird?"

"Jason, I think."

"You *think*?"

"Yes."

"His last name?"

"I don't know. These guys don't use last names."

"Did you see him get shot?"

"No, but I heard the shot. That's when I ran. I figured I was next."

"You ran all the way to Huntington Beach?"

"No. I ran to someone's unoccupied RV and broke in. I holed up and called a friend from inside it. It was freaking hot in there. He picked me up and took me to West L.A."

"Go on."

"I stayed with my friend in Culver City for a few days, but he was scared. He dropped me off here."

I nodded. "Lucky me. Who's your friend?"

"An old drug connection. When my money was gone, though, he wanted me to leave."

"Did you shoot up on my couch?"

She didn't reply.

J.R. RAIN

4.

I was at a place called Smokey's.

It wasn't much of a place, but it served beer, so it couldn't have been that bad. I was sitting in the shadows at the short end of an L-shaped bar, my back to the wall. I think I might have been a cowboy in a past life. And a knight, of course. And, if I went back far enough, probably a barbarian, too. I could imagine myself on a horse, with a broadsword strapped to my back, wearing a loincloth, doing whatever the hell it was that barbarians did. Probably kicking a lot of ass and drinking grog. Yeah, that sounded like me.

"You want another beer?" asked the bartender, who might have been Charles Manson's twin brother, minus the crazy eyes.

"Do you think I'd make a good Viking?" I asked.

"You want another fucking beer or not?"

"Sure, matey," I said. Yeah, I was definitely a pirate, too.

"You giving Stones a hard time?" said a voice coming toward me on my right, a voice that belonged to a young, blond guy with longish hair, wearing jeans and a black T-shirt. That the black T-shirt sported a white skull with red devil horns was a given. Although Michael weighed a buck-sixty, dripping wet, he was a tough little dude that might—*might*—give even me a problem.

"Stones?" I said.

"Yeah, Stones," said Michael coming up to me and clasping my hand and arm with a firm grip in a long-time-no-see bro shake. He smelled of hard liquor and cigarettes and probably weed, too. Mixed with all of that was a touch of body odor and cologne and bike grease. He smelled, basically, like a real man. He added, "I think the name refers to his balls, or lack thereof."

"Lost them in the war?"

"What war, Knighthorse?"

"Seemed like the thing to say."

Michael shook his head and raised his finger, a gesture that Stones saw instantly.

"Lost them to cancer, Knighthorse."

"What was his name before?"

"Phil."

I nodded, picked up the last of my first beer. "I like Stones better."

"Most do." Michael reached for his beer. If Stones knew we were talking about him, he didn't show it. Michael drank deeply, then glanced at me. He was a young guy, no more than twenty-five. But he had seen much, done much, and talked about even less. What I knew about him was enough to impress even me. "So, what's going on, Knighthorse?" he asked.

"Thanks for meeting me. I have a Devil's Triangle question. I assume you're still affiliated."

Michael gave me a wry smile, one that

suggested that I had said something very stupid. "I'm in for life, Knighthorse. We all are."

"Can I see the tattoo again?" I asked.

"This ain't show-and-tell, big guy."

"I have my reasons."

He leaned over and showed me the inside of his arm, and revealed the tattoo I had seen a few years ago, back when I first met him on one of my investigations, an investigation in which he had been witness to a murder, a murder he still wouldn't speak about. The tattoo was, of course, the same tattoo that was on Camry's forearm. A triangle with a laughing devil in the middle. It always looked creepy as hell to me.

I told him about Camry. I told him about Steel Eye and J-Bird, too. As I did so, I bought Michael another beer.

"So, you think buying me two beers is enough to spill my guts about my fellow brothers?"

"I think it's enough for you to help me out, in whatever capacity you deem appropriate."

He thought about what he wanted to say.

While he thought, he drank some beer. "There are lots of charters," he said. "The Devil's Triangle is wide and far-reaching. Hell, we even have charters in Europe and South America."

"Everyone wants to be an outlaw."

"We're not outlaws, Knighthorse. At least, not officially."

"Fine. And unofficially?"

"Unofficially, we make ends meet."

"Drugs, prostitution, theft?"

"The list goes on and on, Knighthorse. You don't join the Devil's Triangle because you're a good guy wanting to do good things in the world."

"Why did you come to the DT?" I asked, using the common reference to the Devil's Triangle.

"Because I wanted to party. Because I wanted to be free. Because I wanted to give the finger to the establishment. Because I wanted to live hard, fight hard, party hard."

"Are we partying hard now?" I asked.

"Not now, Knighthorse. But I can take you to one of our parties. Hell, you just might fit in."

"Maybe another time."

"We're always around, Knighthorse. Always ready to party."

"Does the partying begin after you guys get off work, and end at a sensible hour?"

Michael, with his steel-blue eyes, broken nose, a scar over his right eye, and chipped front tooth, looked at me briefly, then threw back his head. "Never, Knighthorse. Just hearing those words...work and sensible...send a shiver through me."

"Nothing wrong with an honest day's work."

"And nothing wrong with living free, Jim."

"Freedom is relative," I said. "You've been to jail three times."

"Never said there wasn't a price to pay for life lived on the fringe, Knighthorse. If going to jail three or four times is the price I have to pay, then so be it."

"I'm leaning toward that we might have different outlooks on life."

"Maybe not so different, Knighthorse. You work as a private eye. You work for yourself. You take the jobs as they come to you, work your own hours, work when you want to."

"I work where the job takes me. Like here."

He laughed again. "This isn't work, Knighthorse. This is living, bro."

"Kind of feels like work."

He laughed again and slapped me on the shoulder as he stood. "So what, exactly, do you want from me, Jim?"

"I want to talk to Steel Eye, and I want to know about the guy he killed."

He looked at me long and hard, with his own steel eyes. He might have been smaller than me, but he oozed toughness. I suspected I oozed toughness, too, but I didn't think Michael cared. Instead, he was weighing how much of a friend I was compared to the amount of shit he might find himself in by helping me.

Finally, he nodded and said, "I'll see what I can do, Jim," and he patted me on the shoulder and left me with the bill.

Yeah, it definitely felt like work.

J.R. RAIN

5.

It was late and we were both in bed, but not together. I hate when that happens. Instead, Cindy and I were on the phone.

"Did you say her name was Camry?"

"I did, yes."

"I've owned two Camrys," said Cindy.

"Nothing to be proud of."

"They were good cars."

"Still nothing to be proud of."

"And she's sleeping in your living room?"

"She is, yes."

"And she paid your standard retainer

fee?"

"She did not."

"Then what, exactly, did she pay?"

"Nothing."

"And you took her case?"

"I did, yes."

"But she broke into your office."

"She did, yes."

"And she is an admitted thief and drug addict?"

"Yes and yes."

"And you're still going to help her?"

"Thieves and drug addicts need help, too. Now, did you want to start the phone sex or shall I?"

She ignored me. "Is she cute?"

"Is that relevant?"

"It is if she's sleeping down the hall and I'm sleeping over here."

"Both good points."

"Well?"

"She is not you," I said. "So, therefore, she is not my type."

"But she is pretty?"

"In a non-standard way."

"She looks strung-out, you mean?" said

Cindy.

"She does, yes. You have nothing to worry about. As they say, I only have eyes for you."

"You're helping her because she's a woman in need."

"A human being in need," I corrected.

"If she were a man, would you offer the same services?"

"I would."

"Fine. So who, exactly, is after Camry?"

"Her ex-boyfriend."

"Her ex-boyfriend who happens to be the leader of a biker gang."

"That about sums it up." I told her the gang's name.

"I've heard of this gang."

"Most have."

"Aren't they, like, killers?"

"Some of them."

"And they sell drugs?"

"Biker gangs are known to be in the drug-supplying business."

"And have turf wars with other biker gangs."

"That's the rumor."

"Jim, I don't like this."

"She likes it even less."

"But she got herself into it."

"And I'm going to get her out of it."

"Jim, these guys are killers. They're like modern-day outlaws."

I grinned. "Maybe."

Through my closed door, I could hear the TV going. Camry was watching the local news. On the bed next to me, Junior slept fitfully. He didn't like having a stranger in the house. He especially didn't like Camry, and spent most of his time growling at her deep in his throat. He's cute like that.

Cindy went on, "There are lots of them, and only one of you."

"Sometimes, I'm enough."

"What if you're not?"

"If I'm not enough—and that's a big *if* —then, I've got friends. Friends in low places, you could say."

"Jim, this isn't funny."

"Which is why you should be all the more impressed that I can find the humor in it."

"There's something fishy about all this."

"Boy, you scholars use fancy words."

I could literally hear her drumming her fingers through the phone. After a moment, she said, "That's asking a lot of your friends."

"I've got good friends."

"This doesn't include your father."

"No."

"But will you call on him, too?"

"If I have to."

"Your father will help you."

"My father is hit or miss. He will help me if he thinks it will benefit him."

"You're too trusting, Jim." I could almost see her shaking her head in disapproval.

"It's a calculated trust."

Cindy might have laughed, but it was hard to tell through the phone. She might have just as easily rolled her eyes. Which was hard to tell through the phone, too. Once we'd tried using Skype. I didn't like it. My head, in the computer screen, looked far too big and squarish.

"I'm worried about you, Jim. These guys are killers."

"Some of them."

"And part of a gang."

"Would it help if I told you that I'm a big boy?"

"No."

"How about a *really* big boy?"

"Jim, this is serious."

"What if I asked you to trust me?"

"I trust you," said Cindy. "It's the biker gang that I don't trust. So, why did she leave the gang?"

"She saw something she shouldn't have seen."

"Oh, God. Please don't tell me she saw someone get killed."

"She saw someone get killed. Or rather, heard it."

"Now, I *really* don't like this."

We'd had this talk before. Not too long ago, Cindy had thought she couldn't handle the stress of dating me. We had taken some time off to think about it. We came back to each other stronger than ever, but the worry was still there. I didn't blame her. I would be worried for me, too, if I wasn't me. Mostly, I worry for the other guys. And even then, I rarely do. Maybe I'm more like my father than I thought.

"So, what kind of help does she need?"

"For now, she needs a place to stay that's safe. I happen to offer the safest place in town."

Cindy laughed, a rich sound coming through the phone. "You drive me crazy, Jim."

"But you love me."

"Dammit, I do. More than ever."

Although we were quiet, I knew her mind wasn't. And while I listened to Jimmy Fallon coming from the living room TV, some homeless man's yelling coming up from the street and my dog's half snores, I knew her mind was racing a mile a minute.

Finally, she said, "So how long will you protect her?"

"Until she doesn't need protecting."

"How will you know that?"

"I'll know."

"Oh, God. Please tell me you're not planning on taking down a whole biker gang."

"Maybe not the *whole* gang," I said.

"Just tell me you'll be careful."

"Careful is my middle name."

"It couldn't be further from your middle name."

6.

It was the next morning when I got the call.

"I thought all bikers slept in until noon," I said. I was in my office. So was Camry. She was on the couch, texting furiously, her thumbs a blur, the tip of her tongue sticking out the corner of her mouth. I rarely text, and when I do, it's never furiously. It's methodical and slow, since I tend to almost always hit the wrong key. Cell phones weren't made for big men with gorilla fingers.

"Only the slackers," said Michael on the other end. "The rest of us are up early, kicking ass and drinking beer, and not necessarily in that order."

"You paint a beautiful picture," I said. "What do you have?"

Michael had come through. Turned out Steel Eye hadn't killed J-Bird. Instead, the biker leader had royally kicked the shit out of J-Bird, and sent him packing. Word on the street was that J-Bird had a concussion and a mouth full of broken teeth and, more than likely, a broken jaw.

"And the gunshot?" I asked.

"Just to scare him."

"He wasn't even shot?"

"No."

"Just got the shit kicked out of him?" I said.

"He messed around. Deserved what he got."

I nodded on my end. "So we're not dealing with a homicide?"

"Nope."

I glanced at Camry. She was still texting. I doubted she was listening.

"One other thing, Knighthorse."

I waited.

"He's looking for Camry."

"I imagine he is."

"And from what I hear, he's going to do a lot more than slap her around for running out on him."

"How much more?"

"With Steel Eye, you never know. He's unpredictable. It's why I'm not affiliated with that charter anymore. I ride with a different band of brothers. But he's going to hurt her, and bad."

"Remind her who's boss and all that."

"Something like that. Look Knighthorse, this isn't going to end well for her...or for you."

"What about for him?" I asked.

"Someday it will end bad for him, too."

I thought about that as we hung up.

Then I made some calls.

J.R. RAIN

7.

It didn't take me long to find the Pit. I am, after all, an ace detective. At least, that's what I keep telling myself.

The locals all knew of it, although few were forthcoming about its location. Luckily, I have a winning smile and a way with words. Not to mention, you get the locals drunk enough, they'll spill their guts. So, after a drinking binge with two wannabe bikers in a city called Cathedral City, which sounded more attractive than it was, I was on my way.

After a few trial and errors, I eventually

found myself on an unmarked road in the middle of nowhere. The sun was setting in my rearview mirror, and a dust cloud billowed behind my van. Yes, I drive a van. Or, as some have been known to call it, the Mystery Machine. And by some, I meant me.

I heard the music before I saw them. Then I saw the glow highlighting a circular rock formation. Kind of like Stonehenge for stoners. Shadows moved around the rocks. Then again, maybe I stumbled upon a secret initiation into the Illuminati.

Or not, I thought, when I saw all the Harleys lined up. Just a bunch of bikers breaking the rules and doing what they do best...party and piss.

I parked behind a boulder, between two fatboys that were dusty and shining all at once. Dichotomy at its best. Now I heard them. Talking loudly. Arguing. Laughing. Snoring. Beer cans cracked open. Beer bottles being broken. The sound of fucking in the nearby bushes. Or lovemaking. Yes, I'm ever the romantic.

I knew what Steel Eye looked like,

thanks to Camry, and I knew where he usually sat, also thanks to Camry.

So I took out my Walther and stepped out into the evening air that was suffused with campfire smoke, weed, tobacco, exhaust, weed, grease, desert sage, dust, weed, and Ralph Lauren.

The Ralph Lauren might have been me, a birthday gift from Cindy. I figure if you're going to kick some ass, might as well smell good doing it.

I paused briefly just outside the firelight. I took a deep breath and said a silent prayer, then stepped around a boulder and held out my gun.

8.

There were about twenty of them. And only one of me.

I liked my odds.

Actually, I didn't. But I also liked to maintain a sense of positive expectation, even now, even while a half dozen faces turned simultaneously toward me, squinting through the smoke.

One of them stood, rising straight up from a log. I briefly wondered where they had gotten a log in the desert when I stiff-armed the guy, sending him spinning and stumbling back over the same log that may or may not have been indigenous to the region.

Although all eyes were on me, I still hadn't attracted the attention of the man I wanted most, a man who was sitting in a wicker chair near the big fire and talking quietly to a young female, herself sitting on a flat piece of wood that could have been driftwood. Misplaced logs and driftwood? I suspected someone in this group was a closet beachcomber.

She spotted me first, eyes widening. I didn't fault her. My eyes would widen too if I saw me coming.

Now I heard the whispery sound of guns being withdrawn, hammers snapped back and shotguns pumped. I also heard the whispery snap of switchblades.

I stepped around the fire. Someone stood quickly from a plastic chair. That someone got kicked back into said plastic chair, to tumble ass backwards into the sand. Now people were moving toward me, but I had a bead on the man in the wicker chair.

A man who finally looked at me.

I could have been wrong—and the

evening light was murky at best—but I was fairly certain his left eye was washed out, like a broken egg yolk in a sunny side up that got away from the chef. According to Camry, he was blind in the washed-out eye. I might have felt sad for him, accept that I caught sight of the girl next to him, a girl who was sporting fresh bruises along her arms and upper thighs.

Steel Eye was faster than I expected. He was up and moving, reaching behind his back and withdrawing a pearl-handled revolver.

Or, rather, trying to.

Turns out I'm pretty fast too, especially now that my leg had been healed by God. Funny story.

I took two long strides and, just as Steel Eye was bringing his weapon up, I drove my fist straight into his mouth and heard a sound that I knew to be teeth breaking.

The punch was delivered with a lot of momentum, too. Not to mention I had put all of my weight in it. The result was pure mayhem. If Steel Eye wasn't such a big son of a bitch himself, I might have broken his neck. As it was, his head snapped back and he staggered backwards. He would have fallen if I had hadn't grabbed his collar and spun him around. I brought up my own gun and pressed it against his temple and faced the others. A half dozen guns of varying shapes and sizes were pointed at us.

"What?" I asked, grinning perhaps a little too big. "Do I have something in my teeth?"

9.

My punch had been a little harder than I had intended. Blame it on adrenalin. And having a dozen or so weapons pointed at your back.

The result was that Steel Eye was mostly limp in my hands and I was doing all the work of keeping the son-of-a-bitch on his feet. He stood maybe an inch or two shorter than me and had shoulders nearly as wide as me. Both of which made keeping him up on his feet while I held a gun to his head all the more difficult. Luckily, I thrive in difficult situations. Or so I tell myself.

"Who the fuck are you?" asked the girl who was standing now. She had a tasteful skull tattooed on her stomach, the teeth of which were biting down on her bellybutton.

"I might have made a wrong turn somewhere," I said, holding Steel Eye mostly up on his feet. "Does anyone know where the IHOP is?"

A handful of bikers took a step forward. Those handfuls had enough facial hair to carpet a small dining room. Shag, of course.

"What the fuck?" one of them said. Hard to tell who said what, since there were a lot of them and the firelight only reached so far.

"That's what I said," I said. Steel Eye was coming back to the land of the living, grunting and shaking his head. I held him even tighter, digging the Walther into his temple. He was in for a rude awakening, literally. "Here I am looking for an IHOP. The guy at the gas station said to make a right at the dirt road to nowhere." I nodded. "Come to think of it, I made a left at the dirt road to nowhere."

"Let him go," said a big black guy who was, yes, even bigger than me.

"I can't do that," I said. "Steel Pecker and I are going down in a blaze of glory. Okay, that might have been more suggestive than I'd intended."

"Get him," said the big black guy.

"Take another step toward me, and I blow your intrepid leader's brains out."

The intrepid leader was putting two-and-two together. He was also now fully awake. He struggled in my arms, but I was stronger than he was. I knew this because I was stronger than most people. He fought me briefly, then gave up, especially when I dug my gun harder into his temple. Steel Eye might have grunted. Then again, that might have been me.

The two guys on either side of me stopped moving toward me. They looked uncertain. Steel Eye waved them away. Then he tried to speak, but gave that up quickly enough. My forearm, I was certain, was crushing his larynx.

"You shoot him," said the black guy. "And we shoot you."

Steel Eye didn't like this logic. He gestured toward his men to back the fuck off; that is, if I correctly interpreted his frantic waving. The two guys to my right and left did just that, backing into the shadows. Meanwhile, Steel Eye and I backed up against the boulder behind us, removing the possibility of someone getting a potshot behind me. I suppose someone could always drop from above. But that was a big boulder, and these guys were drunk.

"You're a dead man," said the black guy who, come to think of it, might have been the official spokesperson for the Devil's Triangle.

"There's a very good chance that a lot of us might die tonight," I said. "Steel Eye would be the first." I gave the black guy the hard stare. "And you would be the second. What happens after that, I leave to the fates. Or to divine providence."

"What the fuck does that mean?"

"It means God will decide who lives and dies. But not you, my friend. I kill you next."

The black guy blinked. I don't think he liked me. "Well fuck you, asshole."

Yup, definitely didn't like me. I said,

"That's the spirit."

"He can't breathe," said another guy.

"He's not supposed to breathe," I said. "He's supposed to listen."

Still, I loosened my grip a little. Truth was, I heard him fighting for breath, too.

"Fine, motherfucker," said a young guy, holding his gun out toward me. "What the fuck do you want?"

"What I want," I said, and then tightened my grip on their esteemed leader a little more, "is for all of you to throw your weapons aside."

"Fuck that and fuck you." He held the gun out, pointed at my face. A clean shot would get me. He was too drunk for a clean shot.

Steel Eye motioned frantically and, slowly, one by one, they all tossed aside their weapons, Most landed in some nearby bushes that, I suspected, doubled as urinals.

"The knives, too," I said. "Anyone knows that any biker worth his salt has a knife or two. Go on."

They did so. A half dozen blades flashed through the night air, to disappear out of the

firelight and into the surrounding shrubs.
"Now," I said. "Let's talk."

10.

"Fuck you," said one of them.

"That's one way to start," I said. "But here's another: I was hired by a very frightened, albeit somewhat belligerent, young lady named Camry to protect her."

This got some nods, frowns, an inhalation or two. Steel Eye, still trapped in my stranglehold, didn't move or make a sound.

"I happen to take my job seriously, as you can see. Some might say too seriously."

This elicited a grunt or two. I heard some whisperings under some breaths.

Those whisperings might have suggested that I was a dead man. I laugh in the face of such whisperings.

I went on, "I'm here for one reason and one reason only: Your abusive leader, Steel Something-or-other—"

"Steel Eye, asshole," came a chorus of grunts, along with a "dipweed" and a "dumb ass" or two. What was a dipweed?

"Right, of course," I said. "Steel Eye. How could I forget? Anyway, Steel Eye had every right to be upset. Hey, another man fucked with his girl. I get it. But I'm not here to talk about that man. I'm here to talk about Camry."

They all stared at me, faces blank but alive in the fire light. A stiff wind made its way through the Pit. A dozen or so beards lifted and fell in unison. Two bikers were still wearing sunglasses, despite the fact the sun had set minutes ago. I admired their dedication.

I continued, "Camry has decided to end her relationship with Steel Eye. Apparently, she did so in grand fashion, by messing with another guy and then splitting in the night. A helluva way to make an exit, but that's beside the point."

"What the fuck is he talking about?" I heard one of them say to another. Hard to say who spoke, since most of their lips were buried deep within wiry facial hair.

I powered on. "That's where I come in. Somehow, some way, she ended up in my office, drinking my coffee, and looking for help. I happen to have a soft spot for damsels in distress...or anyone in distress for that matter. Call it a weakness. Call it mildly heroic. Call it stupid. But here I am."

"We'll call you a dead man soon," said someone nearby.

I ignored the comment, although I did spot the speaker this time. I logged him away for future reference. He seemed the type to carry out the threat. Then again, most of them did.

"So, here is my proposition: Camry moves on with her life. In fact, I am going to help her move on, with a new name, a new identity, new everything. I doubt any of you will find her, but here's the catch: If I so much as catch a whiff that one of you is looking for her, I will be back."

"Yeah, fuck you."

"I thought you might say that. But wait, there's more. If I so much as see a biker sniffing around my place, my shop, my girl, within a hundred square feet of me, I will be back."

This got some chuckles. These guys weren't used to being threatened. They, perhaps, had never been threatened in all their lives. Being threatened was new to them. Hell, they were the ones used to doing the threatening.

"Oh, and in case you're wondering, I won't be back alone," I said.

And with that, I raised my gun and fired into the air.

Nearly a dozen figures stepped out of the darkness, each holding weapons of their own, and each looking more amused than the other, except for one, of course. Spinoza, I was certain, had forgotten how to crack a smile. Then again, knowing his past, I didn't blame him.

"I will be coming back with them," I said.

11.

There were ten of them.

I wouldn't have expected anything less. Mixed with the ten were two cops who didn't have to be here, two cops who were risking their careers and livelihoods—and lives—to be here with me now. As the men stepped into the firelight, weapons raised nonchalantly, I smiled and nodded at my good friends, Sanchez and Sherbet, homicide detectives with LAPD and Fullerton Police Departments, respectively. Sherbet was sweating a little. He was a bigger guy and the evening was warm. He nodded at me and turned his attention back to the group of ruffians before him.

"Looks like you got the party started without us," said an older guy who probably shouldn't have been here, but had demanded to come anyway. His name was Aaron King, although he always reminded me of someone else. Someone I couldn't quite put my finger on. Anyway, Aaron smiled at me and winked...and I almost had it...but lost it again. Who, dammit?

"It wasn't much of a party," I said. "Until Numi showed up."

"Is that a black joke?" said the big Nigerian. "Or a gay joke?"

Numi was new to the private investigator business. Mostly, he had taken over another friend of mine's business. A friend who had now passed. A friend who had had the uncanny knack of finding the missing. I wasn't entirely sure Numi had gotten over our mutual friend's death.

Rest in peace, Booker, I thought.

"Neither," I said. Numi was one of the few men on planet earth who would make me pause before a fight. "It was in reference to your lighthearted and jovial nature."

Numi shook his head and continued scanning the Pit.

"What the fuck is going on?" said one of the bikers. That someone might have been about fifty-five, with a full gray beard stained with tobacco and God knows what else.

"It's called friendly banter, asshole," said Nick Caine, another friend of mine who'd swung by a day earlier. Synchronicity at its best. Standing in the shadows behind him was his manservant or friend—I was never sure which—named Ishi. I noted Ishi was brandishing what appeared to be a machete.

Sweet mama.

Nick, an old-school relic hunter in the Indiana Jones tradition, was sporting a sawed-off shotgun and a revolver. He was, of course, freshly returned from God knows where, uncovering God knows what, and running from God knows who. Nick and I go way back. I think we had met in a bar. I think he had pissed me off. I think he then bought me a drink. I think buying me a drink is always the best way to soothe the savage beast...and to win my undying friendship.

Nick had shown up at my office doorstep with a friend of his, a private eye named Max Long. Max hailed from a town called Mystic Falls, and he was my kind of guy: tough, fast talking, and good with a gun. I had asked if he was working on anything interesting in Mystic Falls, and he said something to the effect of: "You have no idea."

Anyway, Nick, Ishi and Max were here now, and that's all that mattered. Ishi didn't say much. Then again, I wasn't entirely sure he spoke English, and I sure as hell didn't speak Tawakankan, which may or may not be a made-up language.

"What do you say, Monty?" I asked my private investigator friend, Marty Drew, who now ran around looking for ghosts with his wife and medium, Ellen, a sweet lady who kind of freaked me out. "Do you see any spirits here?"

"There's spirits everywhere, Jim," said Monty. "At least, that's what my wife tells me."

Monty, I knew, was a skeptic at heart. But, apparently, he'd seen some shit that he doesn't want to talk about. Maybe it's best he doesn't want to talk about it. I like my little world just the way it is, free of ghosts and things that go bump in the night.

Standing next to Monty was another good friend of mine, private investigator Roan Quigley. Yes, a fancy name for a thug. In a way, we were all thugs. We just practiced our thuggery mostly on the right side of the law. And, yes, private investigators often stay in touch, especially when we need a little help. Like now, although I wasn't entirely convinced that I needed help tonight, but, hey, a little back up never hurts anyone.

Roan had been doing a pretty good job of disappearing of late. He still wouldn't tell me where he disappeared to, but I would wear him down eventually and get to the bottom of it.

Rounding out the ten was another good friend of mine from Los Angeles, park ranger Jack Carter, who might have the coolest job of all of us. He had a cute daughter who may or may not be smarter than all of us.

"All of you are dead," said a big guy in the front row. The big guy might have been drunk.

"Who said that?" asked Numi.

"I did, motherfucker," said the guy, standing and facing the Nigerian. "Big man with your gun."

I watched Numi step around the fire, slip his gun behind him in his waistband and hit the big guy even harder than I might have hit Steel Eye. We all watched the guy tumble head over ass—and very nearly into the fire. When he was done tumbling, he didn't move. He might have been dead. No one seemed to care.

"Now," I said, grinning at this motley gang, both mine and the Devil's Triangle, as I released Steel Eye who spun around and faced me, "do we have an agreement?"

The man with the washed-out eye studied me closely, then looked at my rag-tag gang of thugs, each wielding their preferred weapon, and each looking ready to use it. Finally, he nodded. "We do, and you

can go fuck yourself."
 "That's the spirit," I said.

12.

It was an hour or so later, and we were at a place called Patty's, a dive bar a few dozen miles away just outside of Palm Springs.

Monty the ghost hunter was playing darts with Nick Caine and Ishi. All three, I thought, could use some work on their technique. Jack the Park Ranger and Roan my disappearing investigator friend were taking it to a few unsuspecting drunks at the pool table. I happened to know that Jack and Roan were better than most at billiards, although I've been known to give them a run for their money. Max Long, the private eye out of Mystic Falls was currently doing his damndest to impress a pretty young waitress. His smile might have been winning her over. Detective Sherbet had left after a few drinks. I was about to make a joke about drinking and driving, until I remembered that drinking and driving wasn't very funny. Sherbet patted me on the shoulder as he slipped out. He looked older than I remembered, and far more tired. I think it might have been well past his bedtime. Aaron King left soon after. Earlier, Aaron had seemed a little too eager to jump on stage for his turn at karaoke, singing "Love Me Tender." That he had sounded exactly like Elvis Presley concerned me more than it probably should have.

Now there were four of us at the bar, drinking, our elbows up on the scarred and aged wood. We could have been cowboys from days of old. But we weren't. We were private eyes and thugs, and damn good at both. I was drinking Blue Moon Pale Ale and remembering fondly my detective friend out of Boston, a big guy named Spenser, who was, last time I checked, nearly as tough as me, although I wouldn't want to mess with his friend Hawk.

Private eyes are a weird breed. We come in different shapes and sizes. Some of us are brawlers. Others are computer nerds. All of us live in the fringe, much like those bikers. We just followed the law a little more. Not always, granted. But usually.

Spinoza was drinking water. My old friend had given up the hard stuff long ago, after the accident with his son. I would have given it up too. Spinoza, the smallest of all of us, was leaning back against the bar, an elbow propped up behind him, watching Max work his magic on the waitress. Or trying to. Spinoza gave the impression of not listening, or of being easily distracted. I think that was his M.O. I knew the little bastard was hearing everything within twenty feet of him. Occasionally, he and Numi commented on Max's pick-up technique.

"That won't be the end of it, you know," said Sanchez, sitting next to me.

"I know," I said.

"Some will come looking for you."

"I know that, too," I said.

"You gave Steel Eye a shiner."

"I did. Gladly."

"He's going to have to save face."

"He will," I said.

"He'll be coming for you, too."

"I would be disappointed if he didn't."

"You look terrified," said Sanchez.

I drank more beer, watched Nick and Ishi both literally miss the dart board. They might have been the world's best looters, but they sucked at bar games. I yawned and said to Sanchez, "What was the question again?"

"Wasn't a question, and never mind. So what about the girl?"

"I know a woman," I said. "Runs a shelter for abused women. She'll help her start over somewhere."

"She'll probably just go back to him or someone like him."

"Probably," I said.

"But you're hopeful she'll turn her life around," said Sanchez.

"With infinite disappointment," I said, "comes infinite hope."

Sanchez looked at me. "Martin Luther

King?"

"Duh," I said.

"So where is she now?"

"With Sam for now."

"Samantha Moon?"

"Yeah."

"I like her."

"So do I."

"But she scares me."

"Me too," I said.

"She'll be safe with Sam," said Sanchez.

I nodded. And while the singers paraded across the karaoke stage, and while Nick and Ishi and Monty still sucked at darts, and while Jack and Roan killed it at the pool table, and while Max finally pocketed the waitress' phone number, and while Numi and Spinoza stared off into the far distance, Sanchez and I sat quietly, contemplating hope, disappointment and another beer.

The End

(*read on for an alternate ending.*)

Alternate Ending

It was two days later, and I was in my office organizing my notes from a recent insurance case—and killing it on solitaire, as well—when I heard a rumble of bikes. Many bikes.

I looked around my too-big computer monitor and glanced at Camry.

"You told him you were here?"

She glanced up from her cell phone. "No," she said.

I waited as the rumbling grew louder. By my guess, there were ten of them outside. I continued looking at her.

"Well, maybe," she said.

"You thought it was a good idea to call the very guy you were on the run from?"

"I didn't call him." She rolled her eyes. "I texted him. Geez. Who *calls* anymore?"

"Get out," I said.

For the first time all morning, she set her phone down. "Wait, what?"

"I said, 'get out.'"

"But that's *him* outside."

"No thanks to you."

A few stragglers pulled in. Twelve bikes total. Plus or minus one or two. And only one of me. I closed my solitaire game.

"Get out," I said again.

"He'll kill me."

"I guess you could say you asked for it."

"I thought you were going to protect me."

"I can't protect someone from their own stupidity."

"Look, I'm sorry. He said he would..." and here, she looked away and buried her face in her hands, "hurt my sister if I didn't tell him where I was."

"No he didn't."

"Are you calling me a liar?"

"I am."

I waited. From outside I heard muffled voices in between the sounds of sputtering Harleys.

"Okay, fine. I don't have a sister. I'm sure you know that. I'm sure you checked me out totally."

"Get out."

"Fine, I made a mistake. I miss him, okay?"

"Not okay. Get out."

She sat forward on the couch, her knees together. She was wearing torn jeans that might have been bought that way. These days, it was hard to tell for sure. The jeans were tucked into Ugg boots that looked well used. She glanced toward the office door that wasn't locked.

"You can't make me go out there."

"I can and I will."

"Oh, I see." She sat back. "You're scared. I should have figured. You heard the Harleys and got scared. You're a chicken-shit."

"It was bound to happen," I said. "Now get out."

"I should have never come here."

"I agree."

"Steel Eye will kill you, too."

"Or not."

Someone gunned his Harley and Camry jumped and squealed a little. She looked at her cell phone for no reason.

"Please don't make me go out there,

Please."

"We've already been through this."

Footsteps appeared on the exterior stairs that led up to my office. Heavy boots, if I had to guess. Camry sat forward. "Oh, God. Oh, God."

Harleys were still sputtering and grumbling outside. I heard laughter. Voices. Boots crunching. Mostly, I heard three or four sets of them coming up.

"Oh, fuck," she said, and to her credit, she looked pale as hell.

"You can say that again."

The climbing boots were now moving along the outdoor hallway that led to the upstairs offices of which mine was proudly one.

"Steel Eye is crazy."

"I'm sure he is, judging by your reaction."

"Why don't you seem nervous?"

"Maybe I am."

"You should be."

"I should be many things. But worried about your boyfriend isn't one of them."

"He's not my boyfriend. Anymore."

"You can tell that to him."

"Why are you being like this? You said you would help me."

"Help you, yes. Entertain you, no."

"What the fuck does that mean?"

"I'll let you figure that out."

I could hear distant voices now. Someone was asking which door. Someone else said, "It's a few more doors down."

Right about now, the bikers would be passing my accountant neighbor and the girl who gave "massages." I was suspicious of the legality of her massages, but let it slide. It was, after all, good to be neighborly.

Camry was openly staring at me. "You think I did this on purpose, don't you?"

"I do."

"You think I *wanted* Steel Eye to show up here?"

"I do, yes."

"Why the fuck would I do that?"

The heavy footfalls stopped outside my office door, although a few stragglers clomped from behind. I said, "I think you like it when guys fight over you."

"You don't know me."

Someone pounded on the door.

"Shit," said Camry. "Please. You have to help me."

I said nothing. I didn't like Camry, but I also didn't like someone pounding on my office door. It seemed...rude.

"Who's fucking in there?" shouted a voice that was, predictably, gruff.

I said to Camry, "Admit that you enjoy guys fighting over you."

"What the hell are you talking—"

"Is that you, Camry? You fucking bitch. Get the fuck out here before I break this fucking door down."

She looked at the door, then at me, and then made a face that might have indicated that she'd peed herself a little.

"He sounds scary," I said, and shivered.

"Shit, okay, fine. I admit it."

"You admit what?"

"I like it when guys fight."

"And not just fight, right? Specifically, fight over *you*."

"Yes, yes, dammit. I admit it. But a lot of fucking good that does now."

"Oh, it does some good," I said, pushing

out from behind my desk. As I stood, I unlocked and opened my upper desk drawer and removed my Walther.

"What good?" she said, and her eyes visibly lit up when she saw the gun.

"It confirms you're a bitch."

Her mouth dropped open. "Then you'll help me?"

"We'll see," I said.

"He'll kill you," said Camry as I reached for the doorknob and put the gun in the back of my waistband. I needed both hands.

"Something is going to kill me someday," I said, and turned the doorknob while glancing back at her. "But it sure as hell isn't going to be some jerkoff named Steel Eye."

I opened the door.

***

I counted eleven of them. And only one of me. I liked my chances. Then again, I always liked my chances.

"Who the fuck are you?" asked the guy in front. The color in his right eye, I noted, was washed out, as if his iris had exploded from looking too hard at the sun.

"Your worst nightmare?" I said, my voice rising slightly. I made it sound like a question.

The guys behind him laughed. Most were over six feet. None were as tall as me. I noted Steel Eye's complete lack of concern for me. It was easy to dismiss a six-foot-four, ex-fullback when ten guys stood behind you. At least, that was what I told myself, since my pride was hurt a little.

"Try again, fuck-wad," said Steel Eye. He tried to see around me. That was hard for him to do with shoulders like mine. He gave up and looked up at me. "Let's try this again. Who the fuck are you?"

The mahogany handle of a revolver projected from his jeans. Either that, or he was just happy to see me. The others, I saw, were packing, too. The guy in the back was holding a baseball bat. I looked at the sea of beards, worn blue denim and tattoos. I looked at the bad teeth and bad attitudes...and did what I thought any logical badass would do.

I grabbed Steel Eye by his meaty shoulders, pulled him into my office and slammed the door shut behind him.

Lucky for me, the door locked automatically.

***

It happened fast, and the big guy wasn't expecting it.

He probably also wasn't expecting to have his hairy face pressed up against the pebbled glass of the window of my office door. I was almost certain that he wasn't expecting his gun to be forcibly removed from his pants or anticipating the sheer brute strength of the man presently pinning him to the office door.

Now, with his flared nostrils fogging the pebbled glass, I heard a cacophony of guns being drawn and hammers being pulled back. Mostly, I heard a whole lot of cussing and banging.

With one hand, I drew my own gun and held it on him. With the other, I pressed Steel Eye's face harder than I probably had to against the glass. Any harder and I was certain his face would go through the glass. Undoubtedly, from outside, they got a good look at their leader's distorted face and the shadow of a gun pointed at his head. Pebbled glass had that lovely distortion effect.

"Tell them to back off," I said. "Do it."

"Fuck off."

I pulled Steel Eye back and smashed him hard against the glass. I was risking breaking the glass. It was a risk I was willing to take. I'd never much liked pebbled glass anyway.

"Tell them to put away their guns and wait for you in the parking lot."

"I'll kill you, man. I'll kill you dead."

"Other than being redundant," I said, grunting a little as I pulled him back a few feet, and then rammed his face into the glass. Something crunched. I may not have been an anatomist, but I was pretty sure I had broken his nose. That was, if the blood coating the pebbled glass was any indication.

"Oh, fuck man. You broke my nose!"

With my suspicions confirmed, I kept his face pushed hard against the glass... giving his buddies outside a good look at their esteemed leader's blood sliding in rivulets down the glass.

"Tell them," I said.

"Fuck you!"

The guy had spirit, which I broke with more pressure on the glass.

"The glass...it's gonna fucking break."

"I know a good glass man." That was a lie, of course. Who actually knew good glass men?

"Okay, okay," he said, or mumbled, since his mouth was also pressed against the glass.

"Okay, what?"

"Okay, I'll talk to them, goddammit."

I eased the pressure off him and he spoke into the glass from a half inch away. "Bros, take a hike. I got this. Go on."

I heard mumbling on the other side of the glass. The mumbling seemed to suggest that they didn't quite believe that their venerated leader had this. In fact, he very much did *not* have this.

"Tell them to put their guns away too," I said. "This is a respectable neighborhood."

"Respectable my ass," he said, but he told them to put their guns away. I heard more grumbling on the other side of the door. From what I gathered, few liked me, and fewer still liked the current direction in which things had gone.

Most still loitered on the other side of my door. I slammed Steel Eye against the glass again. "Tell them to wait downstairs."

"Go on," said Steel Eye. "Git!"

They "got," cursing and lobbing threats at me. Threats were nothing new. Hell, I'd been threatened by the best.

When I heard the last of them tromp down the stairs, I released Steel Eye and stepped back. He turned wildly, dripping blood from his nose, bottom lip and chin. The drips joined the other bloodstains that sprinkled my carpet. *Don't ask.*

He considered charging me until he saw me holding my piece. Or maybe he saw my shoulders. Or maybe he wasn't as tough as he thought he was.

"Are you going to just stand there and

bleed, or do you want to talk about why you're here?"

"You're a dead man."

"That's a start." I glanced at Camry, who was sitting on the couch and not looking at us. I said to her, "Wait for it..."

"Fuck you," said Steel Eye.

"There it is," I said and turned back to him. "Have a seat, Steel Cheeks."

Except he didn't sit. He stood there bleeding and looking menacing, both of which he did well. I indicated the client chair in front of my tooled leather desk. The desk was one of the few luxury items I owned. That it was left by the previous tenant was irrelevant. Meanwhile, Steel Dick didn't move.

"Take a seat," I said.

We both looked at each other. He glared. I didn't so much glare as gaze at him poignantly.

"Sit," I said. "And if you say *fuck you* again, I'm going to punch your broken nose."

He mumbled something about me being dead by this time tomorrow...but he came over and sat.

"I want my gun back."

I put my own gun in my waistband and opened the file cabinet drawer. I half-cocked the hammer and emptied the six bullets in his revolver into the drawer and shut it. It was a pain because I needed two hands to rotate the chambers and pull the plunger back. That would have been the time for him to go for me, but he didn't.

I went around my desk and sat, too. I lay his empty Colt .45 revolver on the desk before me. It didn't make much of a sound against the leather top. I loved my leather top. I also loved Cindy, but in a very different way.

My phone was in the open drawer next to me. I left it there.

"Camry tells me you killed a man," I said.

"Camry's a lying bitch."

"Either that or you really killed a guy."

"Doesn't matter," said Steel Eye. "Does it?"

"It does if you're the dead guy or the police."

"You ain't the police."

"No, but I'm the next best thing."

Steel Eye wanted to say "fuck you" or something to that effect, but thought better of it, especially since his broken nose was still bleeding.

"Don't matter if you're dead, too."

"You make a lot of threats for a man who just got his nose broken."

He glared at me, then at Camry, then down at my desk. What did my desk ever do to him?

"If you killed a guy, you're going to jail. If you didn't, I'll let you walk. So which is it?"

"Are you fucking serious, man?"

"As serious as the headache that's going to be setting in soon."

"I didn't kill nobody, asshole."

I turned to Camry, who was still sitting on the couch and still looking away.

"What do you have to say about that? He sounded serious enough to use a double negative."

She didn't move or blink, I thought. She was afraid of him, but there was something else, too.

Ah, hell, I thought. *She still loves him.*

I was also getting another feeling while I looked at her. I studied her body language...she hadn't lied to me about him killing someone. Still, one thing was certain: she was afraid of him. In love with him, but afraid of him, too. The fear, I thought, trumped the love, but there was still enough love there for her to text him her location. To see him again.

I drummed my fingers on my leather-tooled desk. The drumming didn't create noise of any real significance. I considered what to do. Then nodded to myself, because I like to be reassuring, even to myself.

I pulled out my cell and dialed a number. Sanchez answered on the first ring. "That's more like it," I said.

"You got lucky, Knighthorse. What do you need?"

"Biker gang. Eleven of them. Most armed. My office."

"Be there in ten. Don't piss anyone off."

"Too late."

"Shit." He hung up.

***

They came in six minutes.

Steel Eye spent the six minutes glaring at me while holding an increasingly bloody wad of tissues to his face. I didn't glare back. Indeed, I glanced whimsically with flashes of amusement and mild interest.

The sirens continued blaring outside even as the choppers all fired up. One by one, I heard them leave the smallish parking lot.

"Looks like you're alone," I said.

"They'll be back," said Steel Eye.

"So will my guys."

"You hide behind the cops?"

"A show of force never hurt anyone, until it does. You taught me that."

"Where I go, my brothers go."

"Makes the bathroom kind of crowded," I said, "I would think."

"We've got each other's backs."

"And they've got mine," I said, jutting a thumb toward the door and sirens. "Seems like we're even."

"Until we find you alone."

"Or until I find you alone."

He glared some more. I tossed him another tissue. Tissues don't toss very well, unless you do it right, unless you make a ball of it first. I made the ball and tossed it. He snatched it out of the air and applied it to his broken nose. He dropped the other one to the carpeted floor, where the hemoglobin transferred immediately to the fibers. *Oh, joy.* Another bloodstain. My office now looked like a crime scene. Many crime scenes. Yeah, I was definitely not getting my deposit back.

He dabbed some more while I sat back in my chair and steepled my fingers under my chin.

"Michael said you were hardcore."

"Michael should know," I said.

"He suggested that it might be a bad move to come and see you."

"And, was it?"

Steel Eye shrugged. "People don't fuck with Michael."

"Not even you?" I asked.

He shrugged again. "Anyway, you got

Michael's respect..." His voice trailed off.

"Which means?"

"Means you have my respect, too."

"Now, I can sleep at night."

We were silent some more after that "bro" moment.

Finally, Steel Eye said, "Well?"

"Well, what?"

"Where are the cops?"

"Outside waiting."

"Waiting for what?"

"For me to call them up."

"You that tight with the cops?"

"Tight enough."

"And you ain't scared?"

"Been a while," I said, "since I've been scared."

"Me too."

"The cops scare you?" I asked.

"Nope." Then he added, "Since neither of us are scared, what do we do about it?"

I said, "We can fight to the death."

He looked at me from over the tissue and his swelling nose. "For what purpose?"

"Pride?" I said. "The love of a good woman? Street cred?"

He shook his head. "You always like this?"

"Spirited?"

"I was thinking more along the lines of idiotic."

"That too," I said.

"You going to call the cops up here or tell them never mind?" he asked.

I shook my head. "The way I see it, you haven't done anything wrong. Unless you hurt Camry."

"I ain't ever hurt Camry."

"Her bruises suggest otherwise."

"Fine, so you caught me. Big deal. You gonna arrest me for slapping around my girl?"

"No, but I'll beat the shit out of you and have Camry film it and we'll put it on YouTube."

"Bullshit."

"Try me."

He gave me the hard stare, or tried to.

Then nodded. "Fine, whatever."

"Camry," I said, without looking at her. "Will he keep his word?"

She didn't answer. Not at first. I glanced

at her. She continued staring ahead, unmoving.

"Or I can call up the police. They are, after all, waiting downstairs. I'll tell them Steel Nards killed a guy, based on your story. They may not get him for murder. But they'll probably find something, especially with me on the job."

"Hey," said Steel Eye. "I thought, you know, we was cool."

"We're cool, unless you hurt her. Then we're very much not cool."

"Okay, fine."

I studied him, then looked at Camry, "You want to go with him, or do you want protection? Or better yet, do you want to press charges?"

She shot me a look that suggested she'd had enough.

"Just leave him alone," she said.

"There it is," I said sitting back.

"You're being mean to him."

I looked at Steel Eye. He shrugged. Camry got up and went over to him and hugged him deeply, bumping his nose. He yelped and she touched it gently, kissing the tip and now they were both apologizing, followed by careful kissing and tears from them both.

I sighed and sat back, then called Sanchez.

"What's going on up there?" he asked.

I looked at Camry and Steel Eye kissing deeply. I said, "We may need an ambulance."

"For who?"

"For me," I said. "I think I'm going to be sick."

The End

About the Author:

J.R. Rain is an ex-private investigator who now writes full-time. He lives in a small house on a small island with his small dog, Sadie. Please visit him at www.jrrain.com.

Made in the USA
Middletown, DE
28 December 2022

20578929R00066